The Blizzard

BY BETTY REN WRIGHT

ILLUSTRATED BY

RONALD HIMLER

HOLIDAY HOUSE / *New York*

S0-BRN-536

For Clifford Gehrt and Mildred Williford,
whose wonderful memories and generous sharing
of them inspired this story
—B. R. W.

To Don and Dee Dee
on their fiftieth wedding anniversary
—R. H.

Text copyright © 2003 by Betty Ren Wright
Illustrations copyright © 2003 by Ronald Himler
All Rights Reserved
Printed in the United States of America
The text typeface is Caslon Antique.
The artwork was created in watercolor and gouache over pencil.
www.holidayhouse.com

Library of Congress Cataloging-in-Publication Data

Wright, Betty Ren.
The blizzard / by Betty Ren Wright; illustrated by Ronald Himler.—1st ed.
p. cm.
Summary: Although a blizzard prevents his cousins from visiting for his birthday,
a disappointed Billy ends up having a very special day when his teacher and classmates
must stay overnight at his family's house to wait out the snowstorm.
ISBN 0-8234-1656-9 (hardcover)   ISBN 0-8234-1981-9 (paperback)
[1. Birthdays—Fiction. 2. Blizzards—Fiction. 3. Schools—Fiction.]
I. Himler, Ronald, ill. II. Title.

PZ7.W933 Bl 2003
[E]—dc21
2002190764

ISBN-13: 978-0-8234-1656-1 (hardcover)   ISBN-10: 0-8234-1656-9 (hardcover)
ISBN-13: 978-0-8234-1981-4 (paperback)   ISBN-10: 0-8234-1981-9 (paperback)

"Now don't you dare make a fuss," Ma said as she hung up the phone. "It won't do a speck of good. Your aunt Phoebe's sorry, but they won't be able to make it this year."

"Why won't they come?" Billy demanded. "Our cousins always come for *Mae*'s birthday." He scowled at his sister.

"Mae's the lucky one," Pa said. "Born in July. No snowstorms in July. December babies have to take their chances."

"It's not fair," Billy grumbled.

"I said, don't make a fuss." Ma sounded sorry. "There's more snow coming—lots of it. Now you'd better hurry or you'll be late for school."

Billy didn't feel like hurrying. He stomped along the narrow road while Mae ran ahead. Without his five cousins coming to celebrate, this would be just like any other day.

By the time he reached the schoolhouse, the rest of the students were at their desks, except for big Jacob, who was shoveling coal into the stove. Miss Bailey walked up and down the rows, helping each grade get started on the day's work. Then she sat down with Billy's class and they started to read a story about Africa.

Billy edged closer to the stove as he listened. He had one warming-up side and one mostly cold side. Africa would be a great place in which to live, he thought. It was hot there. In Africa nobody would ever miss a birthday party because it might snow.

"Lunchtime!" Miss Bailey clapped her hands. "You may play outside after you eat," she told them. "Henry and Jacob, you must fill the kerosene lamps. It's not as sunny as it was."

Billy took out his lunch box. Under the sandwich there was something flat wrapped in waxed paper—a chocolate cookie as big as a saucer. "A birthday-sized cookie," his mother called it. He gave half of it to his best friend, Jim.

They ate fast and then put on their coats to go outside.

"Wear your mittens!" Miss Bailey called the way she always did. "Be sure to wear your mittens."

The boys chased each other around the schoolhouse to the back, where the outhouse stood. They had a snowball fight while they waited in line. Then they started building a snowman. Some of the other students helped, scooping up handfuls of the fresh snow that was falling. The bell began ringing to call them back inside, as they patted the snowman's head in place.

Billy had just finished coloring a map of the United States when Jim poked him and pointed toward a window. Their snowman had disappeared behind a thick curtain of snow.

Miss Bailey looked too. "Oh, my!" she exclaimed. "This is going to be a short day. Your parents will be coming to pick you up before the roads get too bad."

Billy sat up straight. A short school day would be a good birthday present. After that he looked out every couple of minutes to make sure the snow was still falling.

Then the door flew open, and everyone jumped. For one scary moment Billy thought it was their snowman standing there.

"Mr. Carter?" Miss Bailey gasped. "Is that you?"

"Sure is," he said. "Come to tell you that the road's filled in with snow. You're stuck here for the night!"

One of the little boys started to cry.

"Oh, but we can't stay here," Miss Bailey said. "We don't have food or blankets. . . ." Then she clapped her hands briskly. "We're leaving," she announced. "Mae and Billy, do you think your folks would mind some guests for the night? Your home is the only one close enough to walk to."

"No, ma'am," Mae said, speaking right up the way she always did. "They wouldn't mind."

Billy couldn't believe it. Where would Ma put them all?

Miss Bailey walked around the room like a general getting her army ready to fight. "Jacob and Henry, turn down the lamps," she ordered. "Mittens, everyone. If you have a scarf, tie it over your nose."

When they were ready, she clapped again. "Mr. Carter, open the door, please."

Outside, Miss Bailey lined them up. "Mr. Carter, you lead the way," she said. "Littlest boys and girls next—I'll walk with them. The rest of you, arrange yourselves by size. Biggest boys at the end. Forward, march!"

Away they went.

"Good thing Mr. Carter knows where the road is," Jim puffed after a few minutes. "Otherwise we'd end up in a ditch for sure."

"No, we wouldn't," Billy said. "I know the way home." But he was glad Mr. Carter was leading. The road was gone. The pond was gone. There wasn't one thing that looked like it was supposed to look. The marchers stumbled and fell and got up again as they waded through the great white sea.

Snowflakes settled on Billy's lashes, making it hard to keep his eyes open. He squinted into the distance. "There's our cow barn!" he shouted at last. "There's the machine shed. *There's our house!*"

Everyone cheered. Mr. Carter waved good-bye and trudged off to his own little house down the road.

Billy's mittens were so stiff with snow and ice that he could hardly turn the doorknob. "Ma," he yelled. "Guess what!"

His mother was standing at the big kitchen stove with her back to the door. When Billy yelled, she was so startled that her spoon flew up in the air.

"Oh, my stars and garters!" she exclaimed. "What in the world—"

"I hope you don't mind," Miss Bailey said. "We had nowhere else to go."

"Mind!" Ma exclaimed. "Of course I don't mind. Come in and warm up, every last one of you. Billy, go tell Pa."

"Well, you're home early," Pa said. "Teacher worried about all the snow?"

Billy grinned. "Ma wants you," he said. "We have company."

Pa followed Billy outside. "Who is it?" he asked. "Can't figure out why anyone in his right mind would go visiting on a day like this."

Then he saw all the footprints in the snow—big ones, middle-sized ones, little ones—leading to the back door.

"Oh-ho!" He chuckled. "We've got company all right."

When Billy opened the door, he blinked at what he saw. Their big kitchen didn't look big now. Some of the boys and girls crowded close to the stove, warming their hands and feet. Others gathered around the table, helping themselves from a pitcher of cocoa and a plate of cookies. One little girl lay fast asleep in a corner.

Miss Bailey was talking on the telephone. "Please tell the other parents they don't have to worry about their children."

"I should think not," Ma said. She sounded pleased as anything. "Billy, run out and get a ham to go with the chickens we were planning to have tonight. Mae, bring up a basketful of potatoes and some jars of beans and corn. Your friends can go along to help. You'd better fetch some canned beef too."

After Billy brought the ham, it was time for his everyday chores. Most of the boys and a couple of the girls went with him to take care of the animals.

They fed the chickens and carried feed for the big workhorses, while Henry and Jacob helped Pa with the milking.

Billy fed his pony, Crackerjack, himself. He filled a bowl of food for the three cats and set out a plate of scraps for Corky, the dog.

"Chores never got done this fast before," Pa said, "did they, Billy? I'd say you've all earned your keep."

"Snowball fight!" Henry yelled. In no time the air was filled with snowballs. When Pa stepped out through the barn door, a snowball knocked off his cap, and just like that, he was in the fight too.

It was dark when Mae opened the back door and called to them to come in. Billy had been having so much fun, he didn't think about being hungry until he sniffed all the good smells in the kitchen.

"Wash up first," Ma said. "Billy, please seat Miss Bailey at the head of the dining room table. There's a lot of room here in the kitchen too. Mae, you and your friends can eat picnic style. I've spread a blanket on the living room floor."

It took awhile for everyone to get settled, and after that they were too busy to talk. Pa walked from room to room handing out glasses of fresh, foaming milk.

"We'll have dessert later," Ma announced. "There's pies in the oven, but we'll have to let them cool."

"Good thing!" Jim groaned. "I couldn't eat another bite now if you paid me!"

"How about a songfest?" Miss Bailey suggested. "It's not every day I get a chance to play the piano!"

Billy was sure eighteen people would never fit in the living room, but somehow they all did.

"What shall we start with?" Miss Bailey wondered aloud. Her fingers chased one another up and down the keyboard until Henry shouted, "America!" After that, people called out suggestions without waiting to be asked.

"Row, Row, Row Your Boat."

"Way Down Upon the Suwannee River."

"Are You Sleeping, Brother John?"

They sang as loud as they could, drowning out the wind.

"Billy, take out your harmonica," Pa shouted. "It's not doing any good in your pocket."

That evening went by faster than any Billy could remember. They had just finished singing "Yankee Doodle" when Ma called from the kitchen: "Dessert's ready. I get to choose the last song."

They all turned toward the door and waited. Ma appeared,
carrying a huge cake with candles that glimmered and flared.
When she tilted the plate a little, they could see:
HAPPY BIRTHDAY, BILLY!

"All together now!" Miss Bailey exclaimed. "Let's hear the birthday song!"

"I'd have baked a bigger cake if I'd known how many folks were going to
help us celebrate," Ma told them, laughing. "But there's two kinds of pies in the
kitchen, so no one will go hungry."

Everyone lined up for a small piece of cake and a big slice of pie. By the
time they'd finished eating, the littlest children were asleep in their chairs.

Billy and Mae helped carry sheets and blankets to the living room, the dining room, and Ma's sewing room. The rest of the boys slept in the two big beds in Billy's room, and the girls were in the two beds in Mae's room. Four little boys stretched out crosswise in one of the beds and were sound asleep before Ma came to tuck the blankets around them.

In the other bed Billy lay very still, listening to the whispery scrape of snow against the windows. Jim's elbow was poking into his ribs, but he hardly felt it.

"You awake, Billy?" asked a deep voice.

Billy turned his head enough to see Pa's tall figure in the doorway. "I'm awake," he said.

"Wishing you were a July baby, I suppose," Pa said with a little snort.

Billy grinned into the darkness. "December's okay with me," he said. And then, even though he didn't want the day to end, he fell asleep.